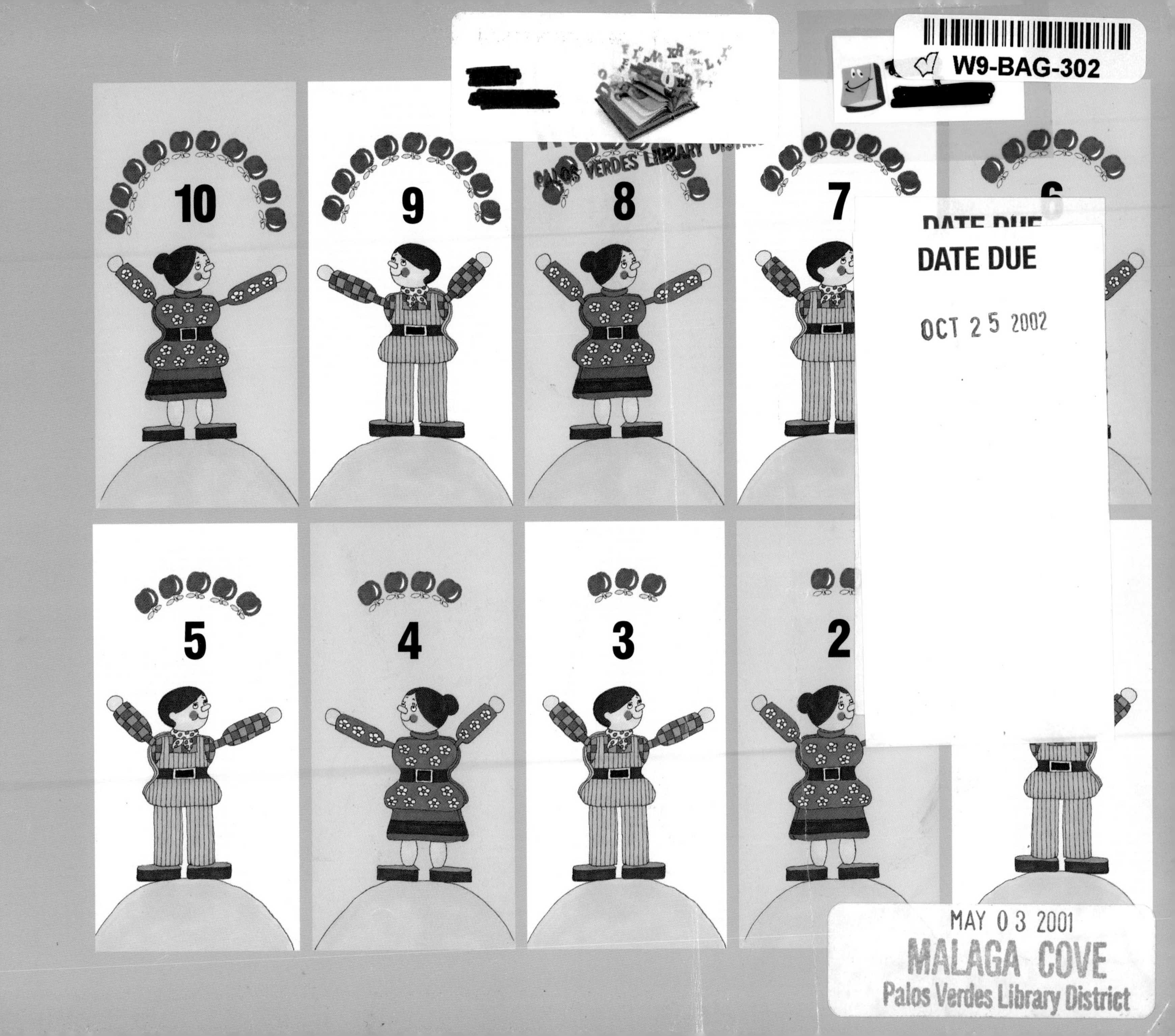
10
9
8
7
6
5
4
3
2

TEN RED APPLES

TEN RED APPLES
Pat Hutchins
Greenwillow Books
An Imprint of HarperCollinsPublishers

Gouache paints were used for the full-color art.
The text type is Futura Book BT.

Ten Red Apples

Printed in Singapore by Tien Wah Press.

http://www.harperchildrens.com

Library of Congress Cataloging-in-Publication Data

Hutchins, Pat, (date)
Ten red apples / by Pat Hutchins.
p. cm.
"Greenwillow Books."
Summary: In rhyming verses, one animal after another neighs,
moos, oinks, quacks, and makes other appropriate sounds
as each eats an apple from the farmer's tree.
ISBN 0-688-16797-7 (trade). ISBN 0-688-16798-5 (lib. bdg.)
[1. Domestic animals—Fiction. 2. Animal sounds—Fiction.
3. Apples—Fiction. 4. Counting. 5. Stories in rhyme.]
I. Title. PZ8.3.H965Te 2000
[E]—dc21 99-25065 CIP

2 3 4 5 6 7 8 9 10 First Edition

For my great-nephew,
Owen

10

Ten red apples hanging on the tree.
Yippee, fiddle-dee-fee!

Horse came and ate one,
chomp, chomp, chomp.
Neigh, neigh, fiddle-dee-fee.
"Horse!" cried the farmer.
"Save some for me!"

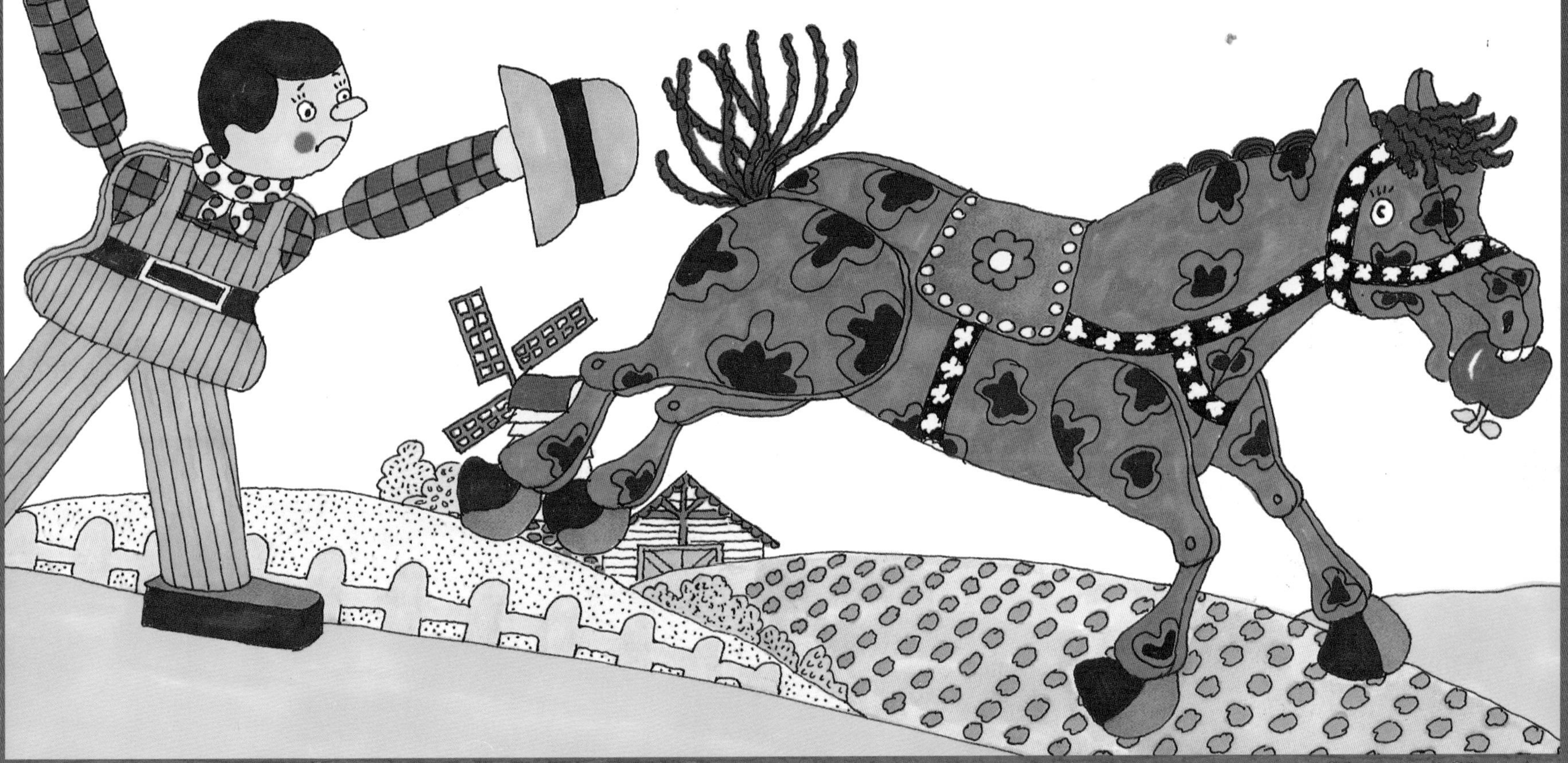

Nine red apples hanging on the tree.
Yippee, fiddle-dee-fee!

Cow came and ate one,
munch, munch, munch.
Moo, moo, fiddle-dee-fee.
"Cow!" cried the farmer.
"Save some for me!"

Eight red apples hanging on the tree.
Yippee, fiddle-dee-fee!

Donkey came and ate one,
gobble, gobble, gobble.
Hee-haw, fiddle-dee-fee.
"Donkey!" cried the farmer.
"Save some for me!"

Seven red apples hanging on the tree.
Yippee, fiddle-dee-fee!

Goat came and ate one,
gulp, gulp, gulp.
Maa, maa, fiddle-dee-fee.
"Goat!" cried the farmer.
"Save some for me!"

6

Six red apples hanging on the tree.
Yippee, fiddle-dee-fee!

Pig came and ate one,
snort, snort, snort.
Oink, oink, fiddle-dee-fee.
"Pig!" cried the farmer.
"Save some for me!"

5

Five red apples hanging on the tree.
Yippee, fiddle-dee-fee!

Sheep came and ate one,
nibble, nibble, nibble.
Baa, baa, fiddle-dee-fee.
"Sheep!" cried the farmer.
"Save some for me!"

4

Four red apples hanging on the tree.
Yippee, fiddle-dee-fee!

Goose came and ate one,
crunch, crunch, crunch.
Hiss, hiss, fiddle-dee-fee.
"Goose!" cried the farmer.
"Save some for me!"

3

Three red apples hanging on the tree.
Yippee, fiddle-dee-fee!

Duck came and ate one,
pick, pick, pick.
Quack, quack, fiddle-dee-fee.
"Duck!" cried the farmer.
"Save some for me!"

2

Two red apples hanging on the tree.
Yippee, fiddle-dee-fee!

Hen came and ate one,
peck, peck, peck.
Cluck, cluck, fiddle-dee-fee.
"Hen!" cried the farmer.
"Save one for me!"

1

One red apple hanging on the tree.
Yippee, fiddle-dee-fee!

"Good," said the farmer.
"You saved one for me!"
Yippee, fiddle-dee-fee!

No red apples hanging on the tree.
My, my, fiddle-dee-fee.
No red apples to bake in a pie.
Fie, fie, fiddle-dee-fee!

"Look!" cried the farmer.
"Another apple tree!"

More red apples hanging on a tree.
Yippee, fiddle-dee-fee!
"Good!" cried the farmer's wife.
"You saved them for me!"

Yippee, fiddle-dee-fee!

Since the publication of *Rosie's Walk* in 1968, reviewers on both sides of the Atlantic have been loud in their praise of Pat Hutchins's work. Pat Hutchins, her husband, Laurence, and their sons, Morgan and Sam, live in London, England.

1
2
3
4
5
6
7
8
9
10